# Elizabeti's School

by STEPHANIE STUVE-BODEEN

illustrated by CHRISTY HALE

LEE & LOW BOOKS INC.
New York

Manufactured in China by RR Donnelley

Book Design by Christy Hale
Book Production by The Kids at Our House

The text is set in Octavian
The illustrations are rendered in mixed media

HC    10   9   8   7   6   5   4   3
PB    20   19   18   17   16   15
First Edition

Library of Congress Cataloging-in-Publication Data
Stuve-Bodeen, Stephanie.
Elizabeti's school / by Stephanie Stuve-Bodeen ; illustrated by Christy Hale.
p. cm.
Sequel to: Mama Elizabeti.
Summary: Although she enjoys her first day at school, Elizabeti misses her
family and wonders if it wouldn't be better to stay home.
ISBN-13: 978-1-58430-043-4 (hardcover)
ISBN-13: 978-1-60060-234-4 (paperback)
[1. First day of school—Fiction. 2. Schools—Fiction. 3. Family life—Tanzania—Fiction.
4. Tanzania—Fiction.] I. Hale, Christy, ill. II. Title.
PZ7.S9418 Eo 2002
[E]—dc21                                    2002016129

## SWAHILI PRONUNCIATION GUIDE

machaura (muh-CHO-ruh)

moja (MO-jah)

mbili (m-BEE-lee)

tatu (TAH-too)

nne (N-nay)

tano (TAH-no)

*For my fellow Tanzanian PCVs, with fond memories of Saba Saba 1990.*
*Asante to the Zimpfers and Yuuka, with a hearty good on ya to Haigan*—S.S.-B.

*For Scott and his chickens,*
*and a special thanks to Jack and Barbara Gibney and Mary Goodspeed*—C.H.

It was Elizabeti's first day of school. She tried to sit still while Mama braided her hair, but she was so excited that she had to fidget a little.

Mama finished and Elizabeti jumped up. She twirled around and around in her new school uniform.

She bent down to feel the smooth surface of her shiny new shoes. No more bare feet! Elizabeti smiled. School must surely be a very special place.

It was still too early to leave for school, so Elizabeti wanted to
play with her cat, Moshi. Elizabeti held a string for Moshi to chase,
like she did every day. But this time Moshi didn't want to play.

Finally it was time to go. Elizabeti waved good-bye to
Moshi. She hugged her rock doll, Eva, and her baby sister,
Flora. She let her little brother, Obedi, give her a sloppy kiss.

Then Mama patted Elizabeti on the head and told her and
her older sister, Pendo, to be good, as they headed out the door.

At first Elizabeti walked very fast, but she slowed down as they
neared the school. Pendo took Elizabeti's hand and led her into the
school yard. There were boys and girls everywhere, laughing and
yelling and singing. All the noise made Elizabeti feel shy. She looked
back the way they had come and wished she had stayed home.

But then Elizabeti's friend Rahaili grabbed her hand and led her over to a group of girls kneeling on the ground. They were playing *machaura*, a game with rocks. Elizabeti smiled. She liked to play with rocks!

Elizabeti watched as Rahaili dug a small hole and filled it with stones.
Then Rahaili threw a rock into the air and with the same hand, picked out a
stone from the hole. Again with the same hand, she caught the rock before
it hit the ground. The next time she picked out two stones, and then three.
Elizabeti had started to dig a hole when the teacher rang the bell.

Elizabeti filed inside with the others. She sat on a bench near the front. The teacher began telling them all the things they would do, but Elizabeti had trouble paying attention. She wondered if Flora missed playing with her or if Mama needed her help cleaning the rice.

The other children started to copy the letters the teacher had written on the blackboard. Elizabeti started to copy them too, but she couldn't help wondering if Obedi wanted her to take him for a walk or if Eva was feeling lonely, sitting in the corner by herself at home. Elizabeti wondered if they missed her. She was certainly missing them!

After their lessons the children all went outside. Some of the older boys played drums while the girls danced. Elizabeti didn't know the dance, but one of the older girls took her hand and showed her what to do. Elizabeti liked it so much, she didn't want to stop when it was time to go inside again.

Back in the schoolroom, the teacher taught Elizabeti and the other young children how to count to five. *"Moja, mbili, tatu, nne, tano."* After a few times, Elizabeti could say the words on her own.

Later, the teacher read a story. After that, school was over. Elizabeti and her classmates stayed to work in the school's garden. Elizabeti helped pick onions and tomatoes.

On the walk home Elizabeti's new shoes started to
hurt her feet, so she took them off. The warm dirt
felt wonderful on the bottom of her feet.

At home Elizabeti was so glad to
see everyone that she hugged them all.

She changed into her old clothes,
which Mama had washed and dried.
They were warm from the sun and
felt much softer against her skin
than the stiff new school clothes.

Elizabeti helped with the rest of the afternoon's chores, played with Eva and Obedi, and helped Mama give Flora a bath. Elizabeti was so happy to be home, she decided she didn't want to go back to school.

Elizabeti went to find her cat. She had looked almost everywhere for Moshi when Mama finally called for her. Elizabeti ran into the house. Mama was on her knees by Elizabeti's bed, smiling, and Obedi was jumping up and down beside her.

Elizabeti peeked under the bed. Moshi was curled up, sleeping, but she wasn't alone. Tucked in beside her were several tiny newborn kittens.

Elizabeti knew better than to disturb them, but just then she thought of something. She pointed at each kitten and said, "*Moja, mbili, tatu, nne, tano.*" Mama was surprised, and hugged her. Elizabeti knew how to count!

That night Elizabeti counted the kittens for Baba and wrote
some letters in the dirt to show what she had learned at school.
Mama and Baba were very proud.

Pendo and Elizabeti danced, and they all laughed when Obedi tried to copy them.

Elizabeti started to show Mama how to play *machaura* but was surprised that Mama was already very good at it. They played until it was time to go to sleep.

Elizabeti climbed into bed and held Eva close. She looked at her pretty school clothes hanging neatly by the doorway. She thought about how good it felt to show Mama and Baba the new things she had learned.

Elizabeti shut her eyes and listened to Moshi's steady purring as a kitten mewed every now and then. Elizabeti decided she would give school another try, but home was surely the best place to be.